# Reg Can Change The World......but should he?

For my son Cole. Inspired by my Great Uncle Reg
and my dog Wilson

Weather

This is Reg. He lives with his loyal dog Wilson and watchful parrot Gizmo

idea for elephant hairdryer
idea for dog scooter
idea for chocolate biscuit tree
idea for jelly trampoline
idea for umbrella hat

This is Reg's favourite part of the house. In his shed, at the bottom of the garden, he likes to invent and make things that make his life as easy as possible.

drill bits

chocolate biscuits

FIRE

Reg loved walking Wilson but it was NO fun at all in the rain

Reg was soaked and freezing. He got his nice warm dressing gown on and made himself a delicious hot chocolate. He started to dream of blue skies and lots of sunshine.

It was while vacuuming up a huge cobweb in his lounge that Reg had an idea to make it sunny all the time

Reg's plan was to go to the local recycling centre and pick up some old vacuum cleaners. 183 by his reckoning if his plan was to work.

Reg set to work in his workshop on his new plan...........

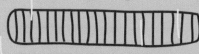

Reg turned on his new super turbo vacuum and began to suck all the grey clouds out of the sky

It worked!!! All the clouds are gone. The sky is blue and the sun is out. Perfect!

The sun was out and the rain long gone. Reg and Wilson were enjoying a bit of sunbathing in the garden with an ice cream and music

It was so warm and lovely, it was time for a quick dip in the swimming pool.
All was fantastic for a while for Reg and Wilson. But then...........

Because it hadn't rained for so long, the plants and flowers in the garden weren't getting fed

Reg's favourite hobby was fishing but because there hadn't been rain in such a long time, the river water levels were very low and there wasn't a fish to be seen.

When Reg was gone, all the local ducks moved in because there was no more water left in the rivers and ponds. The only water from miles around was his swimming pool

The animals haven't had a shower from the rain in such a long time
that they have become extremely stinky

All the shops have run out of honey because the flowers are dead which means that the bees don't have any pollen to make the honey

Because there weren't any clouds left in the sky, the sun was out all the time. This makes it dangerous for the skin. Reg knew he had to change things back to how they were. He had just the plan in mind........

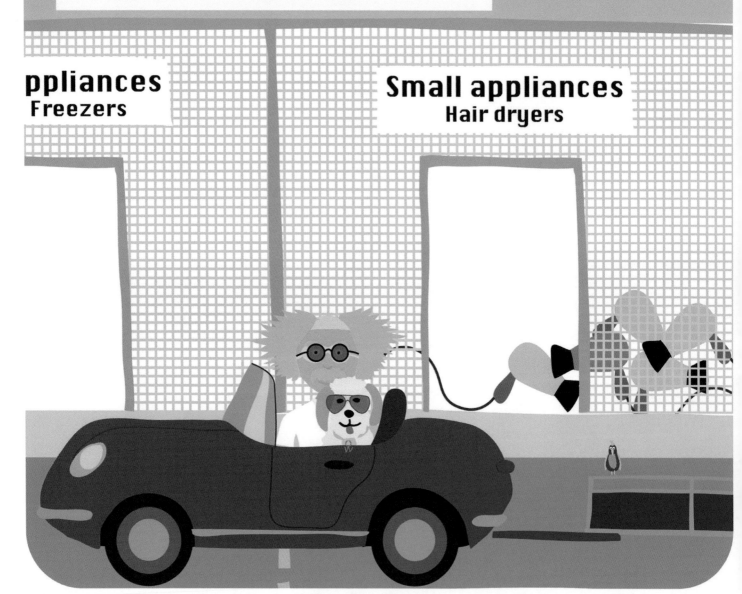

It was back to the Recycling centre. This time on a search for lots of hair dryers. 179 hair dryers by Reg's reckoning if his plan was to work.

TA DA.... Reg's brand new Super Power Air Blower

It was now time to blow the clouds back in to the sky.

The rain fed the flowers and the grass which brought them back to life

The return of the rain meant more water in the rivers and more space for the fish to swim. It also meant the ducks could go home.

With the clouds back the sun had some shade and Reg's sunburn started to heal

With the rain feeding the flowers, bees were able to collect pollen again and make plenty of honey for Reg to spread on his toast.

It was cold, it was wet, it was muddy but Reg was happy.
His sunflowers looked great again,
his lawn was green,
his garden didn't have any stinky animals,
the ducks had moved out,
and there was honey back in the shops.

And so Reg sat outside in the pouring rain with a big smile on his face

**THE END**

Great Uncle Reg and Wilson

Follow Reg and his adventures on instagram  @REGCANCHANGETHEWORLD

or on  regcanchangetheworld.com

Printed in Great Britain
by Amazon

13981582R00022